Baby Self Hate

Luke Hartwell

Watersgreen House is an independent international book publisher with editorial staff in the UK and USA. One of our aims at Watersgreen House is to showcase same-sex affection in works by important gay and bisexual authors in ways which were not possible at the time the books were originally published. We also publish nonfiction, including textbooks, as well as contemporary fiction that is literary, unusual, and provocative.

Watersgreen House, Publishers

Audiobook © by Luke Hartwell.
Narrated by Tre' Nixon.
Recorded and produced by Tre' Nixon and Luke Hartwell in Van Nuys, CA.

Visit us at watersgreen.wix.com/watersgreenhouse

Baby Self Hate

Chapter One

"That's just stupid."

"Cam, that is an inappropriate comment."

"How can it be inappropriate if he says something stupid and I say, 'that's just stupid'? Wouldn't it be inappropriate if he said something stupid and I told him it was brilliant?"

"No, that would be tactful."

"Well, Dr. Anderson, that's just brilliant."

Several kids in the room snicker. Toller isn't one of them. Toller is the guy who made the stupid statement to begin with.

We are in a group meeting for troubled teens. Some of us have been in trouble of one kind or another; others have been placed here by social workers and psychiatrists who think the group can help us with our issues. For me, that would be anger management issues. For Toller, I have no idea. This isn't like AA where everyone says, "Hi, I'm Cam, and I'm an alcoholic." For the most part, we don't know each other's stories. In some cases, we don't even know each other's names.

Toller, though, is someone whose name I won't forget. It's an unusual name, first of all. He's the only Toller I've ever encountered. He's also an unusual guy. There is something about him that intrigues me and also infuriates me. I can't really put my finger on it.

There is nothing particularly noteworthy about his looks. He isn't ugly, but I've seen more attractive guys. He is just slightly above average in looks, like a B-. I am more of an A+ kind of guy myself judging from all the people who try to get in my pants. People try to make it hard to be humble, but I have a deep self-loathing that makes staying humble pretty easy. It's all surface. People see me and want to fuck me or want me to fuck them, but they don't even know me. They just want my body. They could have it, every one of them, if my mind didn't come with it; but the thought of having sex with most of these people grosses me out, makes me wish they'd stop gawking at me. Sometimes I wish I could place my body on any convenient bed and let people line up to fuck it, while I, mind and soul, wander off for a while, maybe see a movie if there's something showing that isn't just special effects.

"There's a presentation Saturday night in the city I'd like all of you to attend if you can," Dr. Anderson is saying. He is our resident group leader, a psychiatrist with his own clinic in Shady Lake where we all meet once a week on Wednesday nights. Shady Lake is a suburb of a larger city. Or a suburb of the suburb of a larger city, if one wants to be picky. A burb of a burb basically. But it's not small. There are about thirty of us at every meeting. Of course, people come and go. There is a new face almost every week, and about every week someone disappears for good. Me, I've been coming to the meetings for seven months. My shrink, who is in fact Dr. Anderson, thinks they are doing me good, and I guess they are, although I couldn't tell you why. I usually feel annoyed throughout the meetings and even more annoyed when they end, but they help. Somehow. Don't ask. I don't know.

"It's a lecture on Buddhism at the Unitarian Universalist Church. I'm not trying to convert anyone. I just think the speaker has some things to say that could be helpful to all of you. I've heard him several times before, and I've always left impressed."

"Is it Tibetan Buddhism?" Toller asks.

"What does it matter?" I counter. The guy just annoys me. And it's not even that he is annoying. Don't ask. I don't know.

"Oh, it matters," Dr. Anderson says. I expected that because I knew my question was something a dumb fuck would ask. Then he mentions some type of Buddhist sect whose name escapes me which he says is all about money, just like televangelists, whereas this other type whose name escapes me is all about living in harmony, something we all need. Yep, I'm going to that. Not.

"Will he be discussing the nature of reality?" Toller asks.

"Are you for real?" I ask Toller, as discreetly as I can. He isn't sitting that far from me.

"What's your problem?" he asks back.

"You're my problem," I answer, because it is the first thing that comes to my head, and it's something a dumb fuck would say. "Sometimes I just want to smash your face in," I add, because that is the second dumb thing that comes to my head.

"Try it," Toller says calmly.

"You just want me to touch you."

"Boys!" Dr. Anderson interrupts. "Please!"

We give him our attention.

"Cam, I think *you* in particular could benefit from the lecture," Dr. Anderson says. "I hope you will consider attending."

I say nothing. I have to pee.

In the restroom I study myself in the mirror, trying to understand what came over me. Why do I act like that? Dr. Anderson is only trying to help me. Toller has never been a jerk to me. It's always me being a jerk to him. I consider telling him I'm sorry when our meeting is over, but any thoughts of apologizing fly out of my head when I hear the door open, look up, and see him coming in. What is he doing here? Is he looking for a beating?

"What's up?" he asks, heading to the sink beside me instead of to the urinal. That just proves it. He's come to talk to me, not to pee. What do we have to talk about? Nothing.

"I came in here to pee," I say. "What the fuck are you doing here?"

Toller doesn't seem like the question bothers him. He takes out a comb and begins pulling it through his already-neat hair.

"Why you so angry, bro?" he asks. "Relax."

I start to say, "I'm not your 'bro'," but this time I realize before I say it that it's something a dumb fuck would say, so I don't. But I can't answer his question either, so I don't say anything.

"You going?" he asks.

At first I think he's telling me to leave, telling me to fuck off, but the tone doesn't really imply that, so hesitantly I ask, "Going where?"

"To the lecture on Saturday night."

I am pretty sure I am not going to a lecture on fucking Buddhism, so I say, "Buddha can butt fuck me," not quite sure why I say it with me on the receiving end; it just comes out that way.

"You say that to all the deities?" Toller asks.

"No, just the round ones."

Toller ignores me and says, "I'm thinking about going. You should go."

I hesitate, then say, "Not sure. I might," leaving doors open only because I'm curious where they may lead.

Toller keeps combing his brown hair, sometimes glancing at my reflection, mostly looking at himself.

"I thought maybe I could get a ride with you," he says, fairly confidently considering that he must know this is the last thing I expect him to say. "I don't have a car."

I pause to stare at him. Another dude wanting inside my pants, I think to myself. What else could it be? Still, there is something about him. I just can't put my finger on it.

"Sure," I say. "If I go."

Toller turns from the mirror to look at me directly instead of my reflection.

"Great. I'll give you my number."

I hand him my phone and let him add his number to my contacts. I'm not sure why I do that. Maybe because I don't want to bother. Maybe because I want to watch him do it. Maybe because for some damn reason I'm a bit too nervous to do it myself.

I watch him enter the information and see that his hand is shaking. So, he is nervous too. For some reason, this makes me like him better. Even if the only thing going on here is that the possibility of getting me into bed is making him swoon, I still like him better seeing him shake like that. I take the phone back from him and walk back to the meeting. Toller moves to the urinal as I exit, and in a few minutes joins us. I can see him glancing at me a few times during the rest of the meeting, but I will myself not to look back. I also don't have any more outbursts. For some reason, I feel remarkably calm now. I still don't know what the hell was going on with me earlier, but one thing I do know is that I will be attending a lecture on Buddhism at the Unitarian Church on Saturday night.

I even have a date.

Chapter Two

The next day after work, I go fishing. The fishing is pretty good at the lake our burb is named after, and dusk is a decent time to go if one doesn't like getting up before dawn, which I don't. I don't have anything against mornings. In fact, I like them because I don't see them often, and I especially like the idea of fishing and watching all the birds come out while the world is still sleeping. Thing is, I just can't get to sleep early enough to get up early. My brain won't let me. My brain is a dumb ass.

I always fish alone. It's a habit I developed early. The usual thing to say would be that it gives me time to think, but that's actually the opposite of what happens. When I'm fishing, my mind is focused on fishing and nothing else. It takes away thought, and that's what I'm after. All the clattering and the clutter that won't let me sleep at night, that won't leave me in peace, evaporates for a while when I'm fishing. It's the only time I'm at peace. Relatively. I'm never entirely at peace.

It helps that I'm a pretty good fisherman. I taught myself since no one else I know is interested. I read a bit about it on the internet, but mostly I came up with my own techniques through instinct and found that they work pretty well. It's cliché but true that after a while one learns to think like a fish, and that's when one masters the art of fishing.

But today my fishing is not as successful as usual. I don't catch a thing, and I realize my concentration's been off. Toller. I keep thinking about Toller.

This isn't good.

Chapter Three

I wait until Friday night to call.

"Hello?"

"Um, Toller? It's Cam, from Wednesday group."

"Oh. Hey!"

"Hey."

"You decided to go?"

"Yeah. I did. You still need a ride?"

"I do."

"Where do I pick you up?"

He gives me an address from a depressingly run-down part of town. I hadn't expected that. Not that my family is rich. We aren't. But I knew from the street address that Toller lived in dark trailer-park poverty. No wonder he didn't have a car. Possibly no one in his family had a car, and if anyone did, it was probably in the yard up on blocks.

Saturday, when I get to his house, I see it's even worse than I expect: Broken down whatever all over the yard. Half-starving dogs wandering around. Chickens. Not that I mind chickens, but damn.

I pull in hoping I don't have to get out and knock on his door. I'm afraid something will bite me or shoot me. But Toller comes through the trailer door before I'm at a complete stop, probably just as eager to prevent me from seeing what's on the other side as I am eager to avoid seeing it.

"Your name's Toller," I say when he gets in. "Where did *that* come from?"

Toller looks at me at first like he doesn't understand the question. I realize I didn't ask it in the most coherent way, but I just wait until reality sets in and he understands where I'm coming from.

"I guess Mom thought she could name me into being somebody," he says. "Fat chance."

"You're somebody," I say. "I don't know who yet, but I'm sure you're somebody."

I'm not sure why I'm complimenting him. No reason to. I guess the "fat chance" threw me because it was something I might say. But it wasn't much of a compliment. No worries.

As I pull back onto the highway, I step on the gas, anxious to leave the trailer park behind me.

"You might want to take it slow," Toller says. "There's usually a cop around the next corner. Speed trap."

I slow down. Sure enough, there's a police car, hidden from view. It seems heartless to put a speed trap here to catch people who can least afford to pay tickets.

"Wouldn't it be nice," I say, "if when cops pull you over, they give you a bunch of grapes instead of a ticket?"

I can see Toller staring at me.

"You're weird," he says.

"Tell me about it."

"I like it."

"You would."

I drive. We don't say anything. I put on some music.

"I like this too," Toller says. Well, that is a start. I had chosen the music with some care, hoping he would know it.

We drive on. The silence is uncomfortable.

"Why you go to group?" I ask. I figure if we are going to get to know each other, we might as well be real.

"Depression. You?"

"Can't you tell?"

"Anger?"

"So it shows?"

We both laugh, and I feel stupid for laughing at my own dumb joke. Then suddenly I get this feeling that Toller might be someone I can be my own dumb-ass self around and maybe he won't think any less of me for it. God, would that be great! Unless, of course, it all turns out to be about getting in my pants.

"What are you angry about?" Toller asks.

"What are you depressed about?"

"I asked first."

"I'm driving."

Toller quickly glances at me then looks back at the road.

"You saw where I live. It's depressing."

"Well, you see where I live too. It makes me angry."

"What do you mean? I don't know where you live."

"I live on *earth*, man! I live on this *fucking planet!*"

Chapter Four

"So then. Anger issues. So, you really did want to smash my face in?"

"Why are you using past tense?"

"You mean you still want to?"

"I wouldn't mind."

"*Why?*"

I look at Toller.

"I dunno. Maybe I don't like your face."

"Or maybe you do."

I glance at him.

"What's that supposed to mean?"

"Nothing."

"No. Tell me what you're thinking."

"We destroy what we love."

I wonder where he read that, but I say, "I don't love your face, man." I think back to our time in the restroom, remember him combing his hair and staring at himself. I wonder if he's vain. "It's a very average face, if you want to know the truth."

There is a silence in which I consider whether or not to apologize. I had intended to shoot him down, but now that I'd done it, I wasn't so sure I had done the right thing.

"Yours isn't," he says.

Fuck. So, this *is* about getting me naked. Fuck.

Fuck, fuck, fuck.

Finally, I just say, "I'm aware of that." The way I say it doesn't sound vain; it sounds like someone deflated.

"So why with a face like yours would you want to go messing up a face like mine?"

"I dunno. I thought maybe you're vain."

"I'm not vain."

"In the restroom. All the combing and staring in the mirror."

"I was just nervous. I'm not vain."

I remember his hand shaking when he entered his number into my phone. That's my fondest memory of him so far.

"Then I dunno."

Toller bides his time. While he's thinking, I'm thinking too, about why thinking *entered his...into my...* just gave me a hard on. *Digit.* That's even better. Entered his *digit* into my...

Toller speaks, finally, and he's still on the same theme. "Maybe there is something about my face you like, and that scares you."

"*Mother of God!* First it's, 'We destroy what we love,' and now *this* crap. Are you a shrink too? I've already got one."

"No. Just wondering why you want to smash my face."

"Because you're annoying as hell. Anyone ever told you that?"

"No, and it's not true. You've got issues with me that I don't understand."

"Neither do I. Stop trying to analyze me. You just piss me off."

"You don't even know me."

"This is true. I can't explain it."

"Well, for what it's worth, I like you. I'd like to be friends."

"You don't know me either, asshole. You just want to get my clothes off."

Toller stares straight ahead up the road.

"Wouldn't mind, but it's more than that."

"Everyone says that."

Toller considers. "Yeah, I guess they would."

"Why would you want to be friends with someone who's been nothing but a shit to you? It's just a physical attraction like everyone else."

Toller turns to face me. I can't look him in the eye because I have to keep my eyes on the road, but I manage to glance at him and see he is trying his hardest to look sincere, maybe even *be* sincere.

"Tell you what," he says. "If I promise never to try anything with you, not even talk about it, can we be friends?"

This is new.

"That changes things," I say.

"I hoped it might."

I think it over and decide to give the guy a chance. No more attitude.

"Are we good now?" I ask. "Can we stop talking shit?"

"I'd like that."

"You got it, man. No more shit."

Chapter Five

I grew up without television. My mom hates it, but she loves music from the 60's and 70's. Well, I'll give her credit; she likes some new stuff too, but it is clear enough where her heart is when it comes to music. So, I grow up listening to the music my mom likes, and I can't help but like it too. But I have issues, as you know. So many things piss me off. And among the things that really piss me off are certain song lyrics. Some are plain stupid; others ask idiotic questions that have no clear answer.

Does anybody really know what time it is? *Does* anybody really care?

What *are* we fighting for? Should I give a damn?

Are we on the eve of destruction?

Oh-oh-oh, what *are* we going to do about you?

How *can* people be so heartless? How *can* people be so cruel?

What the fuck does a person's weight have to do with being your brother?

And why the fuck don't we just do it in the fucking road, for fuck's sake? I mean, *Jesus, Mary, and Joseph*, come on, why not? Give me one good reason?

I would like to take a moment to address that.

Dear John and/or Paul: Had I been born and reached puberty at the time you, either or both of you, wrote this song, I don't think I would have minded doing it with either or both of you pretty much anywhere you wanted. That said, "the road" would not be my favorite place for a number of reasons, most of which are self-evident. For instance, the chance of being run over is much higher were we to do it in the road rather than on a bed or some other more private and comfortable place.

You failed to mention which road you have in mind, and that does, of course, make a difference. Interstate 35 anywhere between Oklahoma City and San Antonio would be out of the question. Perhaps some little-traveled road? I think the risk of being road kill is still too great, and I don't know why we would want to take the unnecessary risk.

Too, is the road paved? I would not want to do it in the dirt or in the mud, even with the two of you. Even on asphalt, the tar would be unpleasant. Then there is the matter of the hard surface, which is why most people prefer a mattress. Even if you—either of you—were willing to allow me to be on top, there is still the issue of scuffed kneecaps. I suppose if you—either of you—were face down on your stomach then perhaps I could balance my legs on the tops of yours so that my knees were comfortably nestled in the pits of your legs, but it is a balancing act in which I have little faith. Perhaps if I were atop one of you and the other was on top of me, pinning me in place, a Beatle sandwich…. no, a *Cam* sandwich; you guys would be the bread. That might work, I suppose, but it sure seems awkward.

Finally, I think your claim that "nobody will be watching us" is highly suspect. How could you know that? I should not like to be arrested for having sex with you guys in public. It would be world news. I don't need that. If you really think no one would see us, then perhaps you have a French road in mind? It is true the French seem not to notice when people are naked or having sex, but if we're really on that road and they don't even notice us, that only increases the likelihood of us getting run over. As much as I wouldn't have minded fucking Paul's young butt, I wouldn't want it to be the last thing I ever did.

I don't think I've exhausted all the reasons, but I hope you agree that this is not such a great idea. I can see why you never performed this song live. I mean, if you're willing to do it in the fucking road, what's to prevent someone from doing you on stage? Roadies? What if your roadies are hot for you too?

It is an incredibly stupid question, and I have to listen to it over and over every time Mom puts on the friggin' white album.

While I'm at this, I'll address a few additional questions, as well. Some of these have always bothered me.

Am I experienced? Have I ever *been* experienced? Yes, and is the second question necessary? If one is experienced, then hasn't one also *been* experienced? I don't understand the issue with the verb tense.

Do I wanna touch, *do* I wanna touch, *do* I wanna touch you there? Um, no, Gary. And no, Joan, and I don't think you really want me to. But did Lautaro Rodriguez, Aurelio Valle, Asgeir, Ilari Peltola, or Justin Bieber ever cover this song? I can think of a few things I would like to do to Justin *there*.

Do I know the way to San Jose, whoa, whoa, whoa, whoa, whoa-oh-*ee*-oh-oh? I realize this was written in the days before GPS, but even then, maps were readily available. One shouldn't set out for San Jose not knowing how to get there. In any case, yes, I do, but I need to know from which direction you're coming. And what's up with asking a question then telling the person multiple times to back off? What is it about the potential answer to that question that frightens you? Even if the answer I suggest takes you through an unfortunate part of Oakland, I can always provide an alternate route.

Am I going to Scarborough Fair, parsley, sage, rosemary, and thyme? Not this year, cumin, basil, oregano, and dill seed.

I don't even know where that is.

Chapter Six

I'm not big on religion. I know others who feel as I do make an exception for Buddhism, which they view as relatively benign. I make no such exception. As I told you, I had no intention of going to this meeting until it turned into an opportunity to get to know Toller, who is making a good and bad impression on me. The fact that the impression isn't all *bad* is new and is keeping me interested. I still like to think about his hands shaking as he *entered his* number *into my* phone. So, while Toller listens to this guy talk, I listen to Toller's body language and look at his body, the parts of it I can see without him noticing I am looking him over. Sitting beside him in the auditorium, this means I am staring mainly at his feet. Looks like about a size nine shoe. The shoes are a cheap brand but look decent. He has good taste for his budget. He fidgets a lot, but I'm doing it too. I like his hand, his left one, when I can see it. I assume I will like his right hand too. I pick out a finger and think again about him *entering his digit into my...* And I wonder how that might feel. Not that others haven't done it before, but I wonder how it would feel if *Toller* did it.

I pay attention to the speaker on occasion, just in case Toller wants to talk about this shit after the lecture. Blah blah blah unity blah. Blah blah blah oneness blah. Blah blah blah harmony blah. Fucking Buddha in the face until I squirt down his throat, blah.

Om.

Chapter Seven

A few days later, I meet Toller's family. There is no father, just his mother and five kids. Toller looks considerably different than his younger siblings and appears to be considerably brighter. I expect they are his half-siblings, but I don't ask in front of them. The family, except for Toller, is what I would expect to find living on this particular road, which runs through swampland east of town, not actually in any city limits because none of the three cities adjacent to it have any reason to want it. Annexing it would just be a drain on resources. There is no tax base here. A stream, which meanders through the area, frequently overflowing to help create the swamp, was at one time a dumping ground for dioxin-contaminated waste. What city in its right mind would want to annex *that?* Leave it for the county and state to worry about.

In my car, Toller fills in some of the blanks for me, although what I saw with my own eyes would have sufficed. I could have guessed the rest. Toller's mother is not too bright but was apparently not bad to look at in her younger days. Toller's father, whoever he is, was bright enough to convince an attractive, stupid young girl to let him fuck her, apparently without a condom. There was never a marriage. After Toller was born, his mother struggled, gained weight, couldn't keep a job. At some point she shacked up with the man who is father to Toller's siblings. Toller thinks they lived together about four years. This man, too, eventually disappeared.

At some point Toller's mom gave up trying to hold down a job while raising a bunch of kids and accepted a life of welfare checks and food stamps. Toller's trips to a psychiatrist are paid for by the state. His mom also apparently gave up on trying to keep a clean house. I have never seen a house so filthy. Looking at all the squalor surrounding Toller, I couldn't help but think he is pretty damn impressive coming from that but radiating none of it. Had I not seen where he lived, I never could have guessed. I still didn't know him well, but I knew him well enough to know he was better than his situation. I could see why he lived in a state of depression. It was already pissing me off. Had I been him, I would have been angry as hell. Had he been me and seen me living like that, he would have been depressed. *Huh*. My mind gets fuzzy, crackles, then fizzles out altogether just when I think I might be on to something.

I listen to Toller, and I want to tell him, "You're amazing." He kind of is. But what I say is, "You're unlikely."

Still, it brings a smile. He knows what I mean.

Chapter Eight

I drive to the arts center. It is a place I go to by myself sometimes when I need to be alone and don't feel like going fishing. I'm no art critic, but I do like art. Actually, most of the older paintings do nothing for me. There are some male nudes I kind of like, though I don't understand why so many of the attractive bodies have arrows shot through them. That kind of ruins the painting, as far as I'm concerned. But the arts center holds mostly contemporary art, and it is always changing, so if I don't like the temporary exhibits one month, there's always a good chance I'll find something I like the next time I come.

The next time I come... Something about this dude has me always thinking about sex. Nah. I take it back. It's not him. I've had nothing but sex on my mind since I hit puberty.

We are standing in front of one of the permanent collection male nudes, my favorite painting from this side of the gallery, when Toller asks, "Your body look like that?"

I realize four things at once. First, that yes, my body looks a hell of a lot like the one in the painting. Second, that I'm not the only one getting a hard on. Third, that Toller has sort of broken his promise. Fourth, that it is a stupid promise to expect him to keep.

I sense that inside my pants a bulge is beginning to pulse.

"Come on," I say. "Let's go."

"We just got here," Toller answers.

"We'll come back some other time. It's just that right now I feel like doing something else."

Toller looks confused.

"Trust me," I say. "You're going to like this."

Toller follows me though the parking lot to my car. Before I get in, I take off my shirt. Once inside, I put my hands behind my head and ask Toller, "What do you think? Any similarity to the guy in the painting?"

Toller looks both dumbfounded and aroused.

"You're fucking gorgeous," he says. "*Shit!*"

"You can touch me if you want," I say. "I'm not a priceless work of art."

Immediately *do you wanna touch, do you wanna touch, do you wanna touch me they-er* is running through my head.

Go away.

"You *are* a work of art," Toller says. "I don't know about priceless. I just know I couldn't afford you if I had to pay."

I think of a guy who paid me four hundred dollars just to blow me when I was sixteen, but I say nothing.

Toller puts a finger on my breastplate and moves it down my chest and stomach.

That does it. I put the car in reverse, and we head across the interstate to a cheap hotel. Well, not in reverse, of course.

"What are you doing?" Toller asks as I park the car.

"I think you know."

I put my shirt back on, go to the front desk, and ask about rates. I have just enough for a room. I pull out my wallet, plop the money on the counter. I have to fill out a form. I make up stuff. The woman asks for my driver's license. I give it to her. She checks the information on the form against the information on my license, tears up the form, and hands me another. I write down the truth this time, and I'm handed a key.

I go back to the car and tell Toller he can carry the luggage since I paid. Toller grins.

We have to walk through the lobby to get to the room. I can see the woman staring at us, not exactly disapproving.

In the hotel room my shirt is off again lickety-split, then my shoes, socks, pants, and underwear. I plop down on the bed to watch Toller undress. The dude isn't bad. He's just average, but I like average. I like small nipples, and he's got them. I like navels that go in, not out, and he's got that too. He's slim, not muscular, but his body will certainly do. I have my first look at his cock. It's eager and cute.

I'm spread-eagled in the middle of the bed, showing off, my cock pointing north.

"Scoot over," Toller says, intending to get in bed beside me.

"Just climb on top," I tell him.

Toller follows my command. I feel the soft touch of his skin give way to the weight of his body. His body isn't the least bit oppressive; it feels nice and comforting. A little too quickly his face is right in front of mine, and he's looking for a kiss. I open my mouth to let his tongue in, and we kiss a long time, our tongues getting the feel not just of the other's tongue but also the other's mouth. We lick each other's mouths.

This is weird, and we both laugh shyly, draw apart, and look at each other. We both smile.

"Fuck me?" I ask.

"Now?"

"Why not?"

"How about a little more foreplay?"

"Bring it on."

Toller wants to lick every inch of me. He does this as I lie waiting for the main event. But I enjoy the foreplay, as well—enjoy him licking my eyelids, my armpits, the insides of my elbow, my navel, my balls, the tip of my cock. He sucks on my dick a while then moves on to lick my legs, my knees, my feet. Then he turns me over and licks everything in back, starting with the feet and moving up. He licks both of my sides, as well. He doesn't miss a thing.

Once he's to my head, he licks the back of my ears while beginning to maneuver his dick into my ass. He's still licking me as he penetrates me. He licks the inside of my left ear as he moves around inside me.

"*God, you feel so good!*" he says.

I've heard this before. I imagine I do.

"*God, you're gorgeous,*" he says.

I've heard this before too, so many times that I know it's true.

"I love you, Cam," he says.

I've heard this before as well.

"Fuck me," I say in response.

He does, and this goes on for a while. I enjoy the feel of him inside me, like the idea of him inside me, like the idea of paying for him to fuck me. I didn't pay him, but I paid for the room. I paid to get fucked.

That's new.

Toller wants to kiss me again. I let him roll me over. I raise my legs above his shoulders and watch him. He's watching himself do me, then he looks at my face and remembers he wants that too, so now he's fucking me and kissing me and telling me I'm beautiful and he's in heaven and he's never felt so good and he loves me and he loves me and he loves me and he loves me.

When I sense he's about to come, I tell him to improve my face.

"Your face is perfect," he says.

"Then mess it up," I insist.

Toller removes his cock from my ass, climbs onto my chest with a knee on either side of my face.

"You do it," he says.

I take his cock in my hand and pump him, pulling him by his dick a bit closer to make sure he hits my face. When our eyes meet again, I feel his dick ripen. He whispers, "*Oh, my fucking god...*" then smacks me in the eye with a wad of cum big enough to serve for tea. Not that anyone should *do* that. Then *splat!*

splat! splat! splat! Four more huge wads of cum hit my face so hard they sting slightly. *Damn.*

More less-lethal jets of cum continue to stream from his dick to my face, neck, and upper chest. I watch him with the eye not covered in cum as he brings his cock to my open mouth; I watch the last streams of his jism shoot into my mouth. I taste him, then he shoves his cock deep down my throat. He fucks my face hard five or six times, his loins slapping my cheeks loud enough to be heard in the hall, then he brings his cock out of my throat but leaves it in my mouth. I'm not entirely sure if he thinks I want this or if he just wants his cock clean when he gets it back.

Toller tastes nice. I haven't licked every inch of his body as he has mine, but every part of him that has been in my mouth tastes good.

Once Toller has completed the ecstasy of orgasm and I have cleaned his cock with my tongue, he takes one look at my face, removes his cock from my mouth, and says, "Oh, *fuck! I'm sorry!*

I sort of want to throw him on the bed and fuck him for all he's worth because that's how I've been used to fucking people— as an act of semi-brutal vengeance for all their unwanted attention, just getting my rocks off on whoever is madly in lust with me at the moment, knowing they are loving it and sort of hating them for loving it and hating myself for giving myself away so easily. I slap a lot of dudes' asses when I fuck them, and sometimes when I am even angrier than usual, I slap them hard.

But this moment seems so perfect I decide to just leave it. Still, I am horny as hell and have to come, so I hold Toller in my arms and begin stroking myself to orgasm. Toller has very white skin, almost bluish-white like some English boys. Even if his looks are fairly plain, his skin is plainly attractive.

I put some fingers of my left hand in his mouth while pumping myself with my right hand. I finger-fuck his mouth, and for a moment I grab his dick again, wishing he was hard. I move my hand around his groin, touch his balls and in between his legs, then his stomach. I make several passes over his stomach with my hand. I put my finger in his navel. I feel his chest. Then my hand returns to my cock. Toller has his eyes closed, never protesting anything I do, although for that matter I'm not doing too much to protest. I get the feeling his body is mine, that I could fuck it if I want, but that he wouldn't be into it. So, I don't do it when normally I would. I just stare at his trailer-park face and his trailer-park body and for some reason thinking of him in those terms brings me quickly to orgasm.

I squirt into his navel, make a puddle, then squirt a little on his cock, and finally dribble strings of cum on his chest. I make it look like drizzle on a delicious dish. The sight of it makes me hungry.

I put my finger in his navel puddle and look at his face to see if he'll open his mouth. He doesn't, so I lick the finger myself. I wish he'd eat at least a little of me. I'd like for something of me to be *in* him, not just on him. But it is what it is, so I get up, grab a couple of towels from the bathroom, and wipe both of us clean, disappointed about the wasted cum. I taste pretty good myself. He should have eaten me. I want him to have something of me inside of him when we leave the room.

I wonder what to say next, but Toller repeats something instead.

"I do love you, you know."

I'm surprised since he hasn't acted all that into me since he came.

"You just met me," I say because I don't believe him. If he loves me, he should have eaten me. This is bugging me, and I'm starting to get angry about it.

"Yes, I just met you. And I love you."

"Well, at least you don't seem depressed."

"I'm not. I'm happy. Ridiculously happy."

"I'm glad."

"And what about you?" Toller asks. "Are you still angry."

The question stuns me.

I decide to lie.

"No, I guess I'm not."

We lie together in silence for a while, thinking.

"By the way," Toller says. "Your body is actually even better than the one in the painting."

"Nah," I say. "It's just in 3-D, that's all. It's real, and you can touch it."

"Yes," Toller agrees. "Your body is very real, and I touched every part of it."

"With your tongue, no less."

"With my tongue."

We lie in bed for quite a while enjoying each other's company, comfortable in our nakedness. But I'm not satisfied, so before we leave the hotel, I fuck Toller because I have to know what it feels like and because he didn't eat me and because I paid for the room and because as far as I know I've never fucked someone who lives in a trailer park.

It feels pretty good—nothing earth-shattering, but he's a decent fuck. I wish he had more of a bubble ass, which I always enjoy, but other than that, there's not much to complain about. As before, he contributes nothing but his body, letting me do what I want with it but not showing much enthusiasm. He just told me he loves me, so I try not to take his apathy personally. I suspect he's one of those guys who after they come aren't excited about sex anymore. I've been with guys like that before. Or maybe he doesn't like being fucked. That would make things interesting because if he was going to be fucking *me,* I *would* be fucking him.

I don't slap his ass as I fuck him. I fuck him slowly, softly, kissing him various places including, once, his mouth, letting him know through my body that either I care about him a little or I just want to give him a good fuck. He can decide.

Even if he's not the best fuck I've ever had, that "something about him" that I had noticed from the start seems quite magnified with my cock inside him. I feel like my dick is penetrating not just his anus but also depths of feeling it hasn't explored before. I feel like I'm violating not just his body but also some barriers I've erected to keep myself intact. I start to feel a bit crazy not knowing what I'm feeling, so I try to focus on the fuck, just like when I'm fishing and I focus on the fish. Toller, I suppose, grows tired of being molested and decides to help a little. When I feel his anal muscles contract around my cock, squeezing me tight, urging me to orgasm, I almost come right then, but I manage to control myself and make the moment last because I don't want victory to be his. If he wants to hurry this along, then I'll make damn sure I take longer than usual. My demeanor doesn't change. Even though I'm even angrier now and want to slap his ass really hard, I still fuck him slowly, no slapping, hoping I'm making him think that just maybe I care, that I can't read his signals to get this over with, that I think I'm doing him a favor by going slow.

I nibble on his nipples and his neck. Then I take my dick out of him for a few minutes because I want to nibble on his stomach too. Then I put my dick back inside him and nibble on his ear. The left one, if you're visualizing.

I bite his neck. He doesn't react.

We don't talk. I just fuck him. He's still pliant in my hands, letting me fuck him and do whatever else I want with him. I suspect he won't like it if I come on his face, so I decide that's exactly where I'll come.

Then I change my mind. I grab him by his hips and plunge my cock as far into him as I can, my loins pressed tight against his body with each thrust. I make sure my cock is all the way inside him when I squirt the first squirt. My cum shoots deep into his body.

There, I think. Now you'll have something to take home with you.

I keep my dick inside him for a while just because I know he's waiting for me to take it out, and I decide to kiss him some more because he still seems to like that well enough. Eventually I've been inside him so long that I get hard again, so I fuck him again, because I know it's about the last thing he wants. I fuck him faster this time, and this time after I come I'm completely spent and want to go home.

I pull my dick out of him, wipe it off, and start to get dressed. Toller starts to get dressed too. Without asking permission, I take a photo of him with just his underwear on. He pauses, but instead of getting mad, he asks if he can take one of me too.

I hear myself say, "Sure."

"In your underwear?"

I already have my pants on, but fair is fair. I take them off. Then, not understanding completely why, I take my underwear off too, so he can get a photo of me totally naked.

"Awesome," he says.

Chapter Nine

In the car, I start to feel a bit badly about how I've treated him. If he didn't know I am an asshole before, he should know by now. It hasn't escaped my attention that he hasn't said "I love you" since I fucked him twice. It occurs to me that maybe I fucked him twice to see if I could fuck all the love out of him.

"You have a nice time?" I ask.

Toller laughs.

"Of course."

I nod.

"I wasn't expecting that," he says. "I thought sex with you was off limits."

"The fact that you were good with it being off limits kind of made it okay," I tell him. It's as close to the truth as I can get without thinking too hard about it, and I'm too beat to think.

"That's cool," he says.

We drive on.

"You should have made me use a condom," I tell him.

"You didn't make *me*."

"No, I didn't."

"Did you have condoms with you?"

"Yes."

There's a silence, then Toller asks, "So you have sex a lot?"

I shrug.

"About every day."

Toller nods.

"Then we should have used condoms."

I can see he's worried.

"Look," I say. "I always use condoms when I have sex, so you shouldn't have anything to worry about. But seriously, in the future, use a condom. Don't you usually?"

Toller takes a few seconds to answer, then says, "There's not any usually."

It takes me a moment to understand what he means.

"You're shitting me."

"No, you're my first," he confirms.

He is quiet, and I know he's telling the truth.

I drive on. This certainly isn't the first time I've popped a cherry, but this time it's unexpected. He's missed out on so much.

"Are you experienced?" I ask.

He looks confused.

"I just told you, I'm not."

"Have you ever *been* experienced?" I ask.

"Isn't that the same question?"

See?

Toller's mind is still on something I said a minute ago.

"Really? *Every* day?" he asks.

"Yeah. Why? Is that weird?"

He thinks it over.

"No. I don't guess so."

I don't know what to say, so I keep quiet.

"For how long?" he asks.

"A long time," I say. "I mean, when I was fourteen, it wasn't every day, not with another person, but it was pretty frequent. For the past few years it's been about every day."

Toller takes a moment to think everything over.

"You have a boyfriend? Or a girlfriend?"

"Never had one."

"So, you have sex with…"

"Just random people, usually."

"Wow."

"I'm shocking you."

"Yes."

"Then I'll shut up."

"No. Don't. I want to know."

"What do you want to know?"

"Everything. Start at the beginning."

So, I talk about my sex life to someone for the first time ever. I spill my life story, say the things Dr. Anderson is always trying to get me to say, only I won't because I don't want to give him the thrill.

"There have always been opportunities," I begin, "ever since I hit puberty. Girls and boys my age, their older brothers and sisters, men, women. People want to have sex with me, and I have always been the curious type, so it only figures that I'd say yes eventually. I didn't say yes the first ten or so times I was propositioned, but the opportunities came so frequently that eventually I had to give it a go. Once I tried it, I wanted more. I was an instant addict."

I look for a reaction from Toller. He's listening intently, so I continue.

"When I was young it was usually, but not always, the same guys and girls. There were a couple of guys in particular, Ricky and Steve. Ricky was the older brother of a friend of mine. I'd sleep over at his house. He and his brother had beds on opposite sides of this big bedroom that was really an enclosed garage. I'd go to bed with my friend, and we'd be messing around with each other's bodies, just playing around with each other's cocks, and after a while Ricky would say, "Cam, come sleep with me." I'd pull up my underwear and go to Ricky's bed. Ricky had a girlfriend who let him fuck her, and he had gotten good at it. Back then, I liked being with Ricky more than anyone."

"What about your friend in the other bed? Did he just lie there listening?"

"I guess. I never worried about it. We were good friends back then, and he and I messed around too, as I just told you, so I knew he wasn't going to tell anyone about me and Ricky. Usually when I went back to his bed, he would be asleep."

"You've had a bizarre life."

"I don't think so. I think it's pretty normal for someone like me. I think *you* have had a bizarre life. You shouldn't be a virgin."

"I'm not, thanks to you."

"You're welcome. Any time."

48

Toller laughs.

"What about the other guy? You said there were two."

"Yeah, the other was Steve, who lived across the street from me. Still does, actually. He's a year younger than me, so we weren't in the same grade, and we only had one thing in common, so we didn't hang out together. He likes all these nerdy things that bore me, and he's not interested in anything I like either. But he was attracted to me, and he was good looking himself, and somehow we realized one day that we were attracted to each other, so I asked him if he wanted to spend the night. He said sure, and we both knew what was up. He came over around eight. We played games or something until it was late enough that we could go to bed without drawing attention to ourselves. We just fooled around for weeks and months, and somehow it was Steve who suggested one night that we do more. I'd never even considered the possibility. He was my first. We were steady at this for a long time. I liked having sex with Steve a lot because he was just as into it as I was and was roughly my age. We did a lot of experimenting together. But as he got older, he wouldn't let me fuck him anymore, he would only fuck me. Then at some point he got a girlfriend and blew me off altogether. It broke my heart a bit, if you want to know the truth. I laid him out."

"You what?"

"I laid him out. When he broke it off with me, when he refused to sleep over, I didn't take it well. I wanted him to fuck me, and when he refused, I clocked him."

"Bad?"

"Bad. I broke his nose. He went to the hospital. His parents freaked out. I went to counseling."

"So that's why you're in counseling?"

"That's why I was in counseling at age sixteen. Other shit has happened since then. I'm not sane."

Toller ignores my self-diagnosis.

"That's kind of a cool story," he says eventually. "What about Ricky?"

"He's never lost interest, but we had pretty much stopped seeing each other by the time he left for college. For one thing, I hardly ever spent the night over there anymore because his brother and I stopped being friends. But we did get together a few times. I'd call him up out of the blue or he would call me. We've even hooked up a couple of times recently. But he's always got a girlfriend. I'm always second best. Or third. Whatever."

Toller says nothing.

There are so many stories I could tell him, more recent stories, but I had told him about the two that meant the most to me. I haven't liked anyone lately as much as I used to like Steve and Ricky, even if it *was* only about sex. Sometimes sex is enough. Sometimes sex is all you want from somebody. I should know. I've been the object of desire often enough. But I'm that way too. I get it.

Toller has one more question.

"When did you start using condoms?"

"A long time ago. The first man, grown man, I had sex with used one and told me I should always use them. So, I did. I do."

"Until tonight."

"Well, no, with Steve and Ricky I never used one. But yeah, for the most part I always have until tonight."

"Why not tonight?"

"I guess you're special."

I realize this is absolutely the dumbest thing I've ever said in my life.

"I'm sorry," I say, a rare event for me.

"For what?"

"Never mind."

I drop Toller off at his trailer park, and when he gets out of the car and stands up, I can't help thinking he looks sexier now that I know his body.

I tell him I'll see him later.

"When?" he asks.

I think about it. I have to work the next day, but after work I planned to go fishing. I need to clear my head. I invite him along before thinking about it. If he's with me, there's no way I can clear my head. But it's too late. I've already asked.

"I don't much like to fish," he says. "But I wouldn't mind watching you."

I shrug.

"Whatever. I'll pick you up around six."

"In the *morning?*"

"No. In the evening. I work tomorrow. It'll have to be after work."

"Where do you work?"

I laugh. "You fuck a guy and don't even know where he works."

Toller blushes and looks around the trailer park to make sure no one can hear.

"*Shut up,*" he says, pleadingly.

"*Toller fucked me,*" I say to the trailer park at large, loud enough to cause him alarm.

"*Shut up!*"

"*I fucked him too,*" I say, just as loudly. "*Twice.*"

Toller's ears have turned bright red. He looks at me, pleading. I like that look. I think that's what I was after. I look at him standing there, all blue-white skin and red ears, and I think he's never looked so cute.

I wink at him and head home.

Chapter Ten

When I pick up Toller after work, he's smiling like the world is fair. I wonder why he's in such a good mood, then I remember something and wonder how many times today he's jerked off while looking at me naked on his phone.

"You, um, look happy," I tell him.

"Yep."

I let it go and drive to the lake.

I feel awkward casting the line, knowing Toller is studying my every move. Yet I'm glad he's with me, watching me, waiting for his next chance to do me. I know it's all about fucking me. He can call it love if he wants, but I know it's all about lust, about me being attractive, and now it's also about me being a good fuck. I even have that bubble ass every guy wants to fuck.

My body is about the only thing I have going for me, I realize. All this time I've been hating on people for being captivated by my looks and thinking they're in love with me before they even know me. But the truth is, if it weren't for my looks, there would be nothing to love. Inside, I'm as vacant as a boarded-up warehouse. Strangely, no one who's ever been inside me has intuited that there's nothing there. They always want more. Well, except for Steve. Toller appears to have missed that too, but I expect he'll notice sooner or later. Then he'll stop saying he loves me, but he'll still want to do me.

A fish hits my line. I reel it in. Toller is impressed, watching the fish fighting me, watching my muscles flex. I'm wearing a black muscle shirt. I wore it on purpose because I know I look good in it, especially when a fish hits my line. I want to look good for Toller because I want his desire for me to outweigh any lingering bad feelings he might have about the way I treated him in bed. I realize he has never actually shown any resentment. It occurs to me that perhaps the negativity is only in *my* head, not his. Toller hasn't said anything negative.

I lay the fish out on the rocks. It's over a foot long. Not bad for this lake.

I take the hook out of its mouth and throw it back in.

"Catch and release," Toller says, letting me know he knows some fishing terminology.

"Yep, that's what I usually do."

Toller catches the double entendre and doesn't like it.

"Relax," I tell him. "I said usually. You wouldn't be here now if that was my intention."

Toller does relax, and something in his face lets me know that he's never had a negative thought about me, not in the group meetings when I treated him like shit, not in bed when I took my pleasure. Never. He's in too deep. I likely could treat him like shit in quite a few ways for quite a long while and he'd still love me as long as I was letting him fuck me.

I realize I'm his dream come true.

People shouldn't give up on their dreams.

I start to put some more bait on my line but change my mind.

"You still think you love me?" I ask.

"I know I do."

"You don't know anything."

"I know I do, and I'll prove it."

"How are you going to do that?"

He doesn't know what to say. Finally, he just says, "In bed."

Of course. In bed. Fucking the symbol of all I am—an asshole. Fuck my hole, fuck my whole. *Fuck me. Fuck me. Fuck me.* It may be all I'm good for.

Still, laid out naked on clean sheets, I'm about all a person could want when it comes to sex.

That's something, I guess. At least while I'm young.

Toller sees me frowning.

"Cam," he says. "*I love you.*"

Maybe he does, I think to myself, but I'll fuck it out of him eventually.

Chapter Eleven

The following day, my normal life continues, but with a twist. I get the usual nods and winks. I see people of all ages and both sexes watching me as I walk down the street. People try to strike up conversations. As usual, I ignore the biggest part of it all. But someone grabs my attention at some point—a guy about my age, maybe a year or two older. This is the usual pattern. It's usually a guy I end up with; I much prefer guys. And I give this guy the usual encouraging nod before I even think about it. It's a reflex. He walks over and makes a stab at conversation. He's attractive, clean cut, possibly military but not in uniform. He smells good. I can see the contours of his body through his shirt.

He looks around nervously.

Why not? I'm thinking. I like guys like this. Like to fuck them, anyway.

He smiles bashfully at me. He's adorable.

But there's this guy in my head who for some new reason I'd rather be with now than just some random fuck, even an unusually hot random fuck. I'm beginning to think I've had just about enough of those. Time for something new.

Could I be monogamous for a while just to see what it feels like? It's worth a try.

"What's up?" the guy asks.

"Not much."

He takes a good look at me now that he's up close, and I can see that he's more than pleased. But I want to end this conversation before it gets off the ground. As I try to figure out how to do that, the guy takes a step toward me, invading my American personal space zone.

We're face to face now, and he is definitely hot, but I haven't changed my mind about exiting the situation.

"Do you know the way to San Jose?" I ask him.

"Say *what?*" He looks confused.

I begin to walk. He hesitates, then begins to follow.

"Whoa, whoa, whoa, whoa, whoa oh *ee* oh oh," I say, turning and putting my hand out to stop him.

The guy stares at me, says, "I should be going," and walks off. This is cool. I'm not used to people walking away from me. I watch his sexy beauty disappear down the street and know I could have fucked that, or at the very least been fucked by that. Sorry dude. It's just that there's someone waiting, someone who's probably got his phone out right now staring at my naked body.

I want to have sex with Toller again.

That's new.

I want to fuck Toller. I want to fuck him first this time so he'll be into it more and maybe feel like his god is making love to him on Mount Olympus. I want to continue to be his god, to feel like his god.

That's new.

I want to experience the exquisite feeling of naked ass-skin surrounding my dick instead of fucking rubber, and if I stop having sex with other people, Toller and I can bareback every time. I feel like I can trust him, if only he will trust me.

I want Toller to fuck me and fuck me and fuck me and fuck me and fuck me and lick me all over again, maybe twice this time, maybe lick me so long that I come just from being licked.

I want to have sex with Toller.

I want Toller.

Chapter Twelve

I give Toller a call, and within twenty minutes I'm at the trailer park picking him up.

"Hey," I say.

"Hey," he says back at me, smiling broadly and handing me a small sack.

I open it. Grapes.

"Thanks," I say, meaning it.

He smiles, pleased to have pleased me.

"What do you want to do?" I ask, eating a grape.

"Whatever," he says.

"Let's have sex again," I say. "But this time I go first."

"Sure," he says, still smiling.

Good. But where to go?

As far as I can tell, there are only a few benefits to doing it with older men, but they are pretty good benefits. Often, they have a place to go, and if they don't, they can usually afford a hotel room. Sometimes they offer money even though I never ask for money. And sometimes when I need the money, I take it.

But Toller has no money, and I can't afford another room.

Reading my mind, Toller asks, "Where can we go?"

I don't know the answer, so I sing, as much like the original as I can muster, "Why don't we do it in the road?"

Toller looks at me like I'm crazy, the second time a person has looked at me this way in the past hour, but I just sing the second line, which is the same as the first with a slightly different emphasis.

"Why don't we do it in the *ro-o-oad?*"

"You're not *that* hot," Toller says.

This stops me cold. I look at him blankly.

He laughs.

"Just kidding," he says. "Which road?"

Books by Luke Hartwell

Atom Heart John Beloved

Nathan's Story

Michael

Baby Self Hate

Love Underneath

Desire

watersgreen.wix.com/watersgreenhouse

Watersgreen House is an independent international book publisher with editorial staff in the UK and USA. One of our aims at Watersgreen House is to showcase same-sex affection in works by important gay and bisexual authors in ways which were not possible at the time the books were originally published. We also publish nonfiction, including textbooks, as well as contemporary fiction that is literary, unusual, and provocative.